MW01044852

Pretty Cat

Written by Marilyn Pitt & Jane Hileman
Illustrated by John Bianchi

I have a brush.

Do you like this?

I have a bow.

Do you like this?

Here is a necklace.

Do you like that?

Here is lipstick.

You will like lipstick.

Look at you.
Do you like it?

Come here! Come here!
I have a hat for you.

There you are, my pretty cat!